My Story

A chapter book by Vanessa Elder
Based on the motion picture from Walt Disney Pictures
Screenplay by John Hughes and Bill Walsh
Produced by John Hughes and Ricardo Mestres
Directed by Les Mayfield

Disney
PRESS

New York

Contents

Chapter One

The Creation

The first words I ever heard were "Wow! What a bang!" And suddenly, I was alive.

I oozed out into the world for the first time. The air on my skin felt delicious. Ticklish.

Fingers picked me up. They seemed friendly. I curled closer and was lifted into the air. It felt good to be stretched out.

Ah! And the feeling of being dropped. I came into contact with something smooth and hard—the floor—and suddenly I exploded with motion.

I'd found my calling. I was born to bounce.

My creator squeaked and squawked. I knew that he was as happy with me as I was with myself.

But suddenly a flash of light exploded around me. I had to escape. As I hit the basement walls I realized I was trapped.

I wanted to be free, to bounce as high and as far as I pleased. The more I bounced around the room, the more it became like an itch.

I bounced frantically until I found a place where the floor rose into the air a little bit at a time. Stairs, of course. I bounced higher and higher. And then I bounced against something clear and smooth and hard that gave way around me with a crash.

Freedom! There was no limit to how high I could bounce. There was only the sky above me and the ground below. I felt like nothing could stop me.

I burst through another smooth, hard surface. Glass, it's called. There were other humans making singing sounds. Screamy, scared, nervous sounds. I kept on going

I sailed through a window screen. My whole self splatted against it, and I separated into tiny pieces.

It didn't hurt a bit! In fact, it felt delightful to be bouncing in lots of different places at once. I could be everywhere—or almost everywhere—at the same time! Each bit of me was aware of every other bit.

Then an angry creature, shaped like my creator, swatted at me frantically. Suddenly he jumped on me, as if to stamp out my life.

He went flying to one side and crashed into a wall. I almost felt sorry for him. But he looked so funny I wanted to laugh.

It was time to be moving on. I bounced back to the creature that made me.

Oof! The next thing I knew, I had crashed through another window. My creator caught me in some sort of mitt—a catcher's mitt. He crowed triumphantly, happy that I had come back to him.

4

"You know what we've got here?" he cried.

"Flying rubber," a strange, metallic voice replied. It was the thing that had flashed that powerful light at me—Weebo, the Professor's robot.

"Flying rubber?" the Professor replied. "That's right. That's what it is! Flubber!"

I snapped back and slammed into my creator's head, knocking him off his feet. But he held tight.

Chapter Two

Back in Prison

The Professor wrestled me back into my dark little prison. Everything was dark, and I was lonely.

Suddenly—I'm not sure how much later—I woke up to the sound of the Professor's voice.

"Keep your fingers crossed, Weebo," he said.

And then I was bombarded with some sort of rays—rays that wanted to control me. Slowly, slowly, I rose into the air.

"It works!" the Professor announced proudly.

An alarm sounded.

"The wedding!" the Professor cried. "I have to go, Weebo."

She remained silent. The Professor seemed puzzled.

Finally, Weebo spoke. "You missed it. It's now 6:30 in the *morning*."

I wondered what on earth they were talking about.

Later that morning, the Professor took me to Medfield College, where he teaches. He brought me into a place where an attractive human sat behind a desk.

7

"Evening, Sara," the Professor said.

"You have a lot of nerve showing your face around here," she said angrily.

She wasn't happy to see him.

"Can I explain what happened?" the Professor asked. Suddenly I felt sorry for him. I wiggled, trying to tell him I sympathized.

"There's nothing to explain," Sara said. "For the third time you left me standing at the altar."

"This is why I didn't make it last night!" the Professor exclaimed. And with those words he drew me out of his pocket. I stood up proudly.

"Flubber!" he announced.

"Flubber?" Sara asked, dumbfounded.

The Professor went on to explain, but Sara didn't seem impressed. I couldn't understand why she didn't realize how wonderful I was.

"Isn't it remarkable?" the Professor cried.

I decided to show Sara exactly what I was made of, but she turned away and missed my demonstration!

"What's remarkable," Sara said, turning back, "is that I ever fell in love with you. You broke my heart so that you could stay home and make a ball of green goo."

Ouch! I was much more than a ball of goo! It was time for me to go where I was appreciated.

"Flubber can save the college," the Professor explained. "Let me demonstrate."

"No," Sara said.

"It won't take a minute," he insisted.

He put me in his back pocket and climbed up on the windowsill. I wasn't sure what he was up to, but maybe I could get away. All this talk was boring me.

"When I hit the ground," he said, "the Flubber will send me right back up, unharmed. Watch."

"Are you nuts?" Sara cried.

The Professor grinned. I squirmed around in his back pocket.

"I'll be right back," he said.

With that, he dropped out of the window, bottom first.

Finally, I could escape! I shot out of his pocket as he fell, and I bounced all the way back home. It was great to be bouncing again.

Chapter Three

Flubber Flies

Later on, the Professor decided to rub me on various round objects.

"Flubber appears to have certain sporting applications," the Professor said.

What that meant, I had no idea. But I certainly did my part, sticking to a golf ball

and a bowling ball and bouncing my heart out.

Even more fun was driving two large humans crazy. I didn't know who they were at the time, but I knew they had no business being in the Professor's house. They were spies.

The Professor wasn't even aware that these guys were snooping or that I was konking them in the head repeatedly.

Later that day, the Professor decided to make his old car fly.

I had seen cars in my travels. They were heavy, smelly things that rolled speedily along the streets. And when they collided, they most certainly did not bounce.

The Professor put me in a tank inside his car. Then he bombarded me with the rays—only this time, there seemed to be a purpose to the whole thing.

"I connected the accelerator to the sliding shutter," he explained. "When I press down, I release more gamma rays."

He got into the car. "I think it will work," he announced. "You want to go for a ride?"

Weebo zipped eagerly into the passenger seat.

Flying was lovely. I decided that I didn't

mind being bombarded with gamma rays if it meant I could fly.

Unfortunately, we only go where the Professor takes us—but I'm learning to accept this as part of the flying bargain. Now I just relax and enjoy the ride.

At first the Professor had a problem controlling the car. We nearly rammed into a house. Then we landed right in an apple tree.

"Sorry!" The Professor called to the frightened little human who had witnessed the crash. "First time flyer!"

Now when he flies, I have complete— well, almost complete—confidence in his abilities.

At one point we soared so high into the sky that we were clear above the clouds.

"Look at that, Weebo," the Professor said. "All the world below and beyond. The stillness, the solitude, . . . the silence."

He turned off the motor and let out a deep, satisfied sigh.

And then we fell like a stone. It felt wonderful!

I couldn't wait to hit the ground so we could bounce up into the clouds again! At the last moment the Professor prevented us from slamming into the ground. We shot smoothly into the sky once again.

That was fun.

The Professor decided to visit Sara, and we hovered above her house. Both he and Weebo were suddenly full of tension and anger.

And then I understood why. Sara was with another man. Wilson Croft.

16

"This night was made for us," Wilson said.

"It's so hot and sticky," Sara complained.

"Exactly," Wilson replied.

"It's such a pleasure to spend an evening with you without having Brainard hovering over us," Wilson said. Little did he know!

"I have to say good-night," Sara said. "I have a busy day tomorrow."

I breathed a sigh of relief.

After Sara went inside, Wilson pumped his fist in the air.

"I can't lose. She's mine!" he cried. What a jerk!

The Professor beaned him in the head with an apple.

Finally we sailed home. The Professor was quiet and sad the whole way.

"I wish I could make you feel better," Weebo said.

"So do I," the Professor replied. "But this is something I have to deal with alone."

Chapter Four

Weebo Says Hello

The next morning, the Professor stuck little blobs of me on small metal tacks. I didn't know why.

"You're sure that the Flubber was fully fixed on the tacks before we painted?" he asked Weebo.

"Positive," she replied.

"And the wear-out time on the paint?"

"Thirty minutes," she said, as if they'd been through this thirty times.

"If the Flubber worked immediately, it

would look a little suspicious," he explained.

"Duh," she replied.

He picked up one of the tacks and spoke to me.

"Don't fail me," he said. It was as if he were counting on me to save the world.

I knew then that if I came into contact with anything smooth and hard, I had to do my thing. Bounce.

Before the Professor flew off to the game, he gave Weebo a parting order: "Make sure the Flubber stays in the tank."

So, for the rest of the day, the rest of me remained locked up. For a motion-loving creature like me, it was horrible!

But then I sensed Weebo hovering near me. I whined. We didn't speak the same language, but certain sounds are universal. But would she listen to me? Would she let me out?

To my amazement, I heard a whooshing sound. My prison was being un-locked!

I oozed out cautiously. Sure enough, there

was Weebo. She seemed a bit scared, too.

I decided to take a leap of faith. I had the feeling that if anyone could understand me, it would be Weebo.

I decided to test her.

"What do you want?" I demanded.

"What do you want?" she snapped back, imitating me perfectly.

"I want to be friends," I said.

To my amazement, Weebo understood me! She even answered me in my own language. "Well, I want to be your friend, too. I'll let you out, under one condition."

"What?" I cried.

"You agree to play with me."

"Sure!" I replied joyfully.

"Come on out," she said. "The Professor went to the basketball game."

I knew that, of course, since part of me was with him.

"All right!" I said. I poked my head out and looked right into Weebo's camera eye.

Suddenly, I saw my reflection and reared back. I'd never seen myself before. Was she trying to trick me? I wondered.

I tried to poke her in the lenses, and she snapped them shut.

I reverted to my regular, round shape and chuckled. Then Weebo flashed one of her terrifying flashes of light. I screamed and took off.

I bounced around like a maniac and finally found the stairs. I had to get away from that light and from that godforsaken basement.

When I got upstairs, I calmed down. I

decided to play a game of hide-and-seek. I bounced onto a table and into a box. She'll never find me here, I thought.

I held my breath and kept perfectly still. Eventually, I heard Weebo zip out. She was scanning the room for me. I peeked out of the box for a moment.

The next time I peeked out, she was right there. She'd found me, all right.

"Hello," she said, her voice friendly. The last of my fear disappeared.

Chapter Five

It's Party Time

Meanwhile, the little bits of me found themselves at the basketball court, stuck underneath hot rubbery things. People were yelling and screaming. It was kind of hard to tell if they were happy or mad.

The boys on the court were playing a game involving a ball and two hoops and lots of running and jumping.

Unfortunately, Medfield's players were very short. It was clear they'd never win the game without my help. The Rutland Rangers didn't jump very high, by my standards, but they were jumping giants compared to the Medfield Squirrels.

I couldn't bounce right away because of the sticky substance covering me. But when it wore off, I started bouncing up a storm.

Suddenly, the Medfield Squirrels were leaping all over the place and stuffing the ball in the hoop. I bounced even higher with excitement.

26

"They're doing something illegal!" Rutland's coach screamed.

"Nowhere in the rule book does it say anything about jumping too high," the referee yelled back.

Thanks to me, the Squirrels did the impossible. They beat the Rangers. I was very happy, and the Professor was, too.

"We won!" he yelled, and gave Sara a big hug.

* * *

Back at home, Weebo and I were playing a game of our own. We wanted to have the kind of fun we could only have while the Professor was away.

Weebo put on some rollicking music with an amazing beat.

Music is something I'd never heard until that moment. I went crazy. I just loved it.

I felt happiness surge through me. I already knew I loved to bounce, but I learned that night that I also loved to dance.

The whole house rocked to the beat, and Weebo and I danced up a storm.

I bounced, rose up in the air, wiggled, stretched, and turned into many dancers— I did everything I could think of. And Weebo was a great dancer, too. She spun, rocked, swooped, and rolled end-over-end.

Then she zipped into the kitchen. She pointed herself at the appliances—the dishwasher, the blender, the popcorn popper—and turned them all on. They added their sounds to the music—rolling back and forth, squirting, blending, popping, whooshing. Everything mechanical in the entire house was dancing to the music.

Then Weebo created a small pool of light on the floor. I knew it was meant just for me.

I slapped down onto the floor and started dancing like I'd seen the humans do in Weebo's videos. First I was one dancer, but I kept turning into more. Finally there were sixty-four of me dancing in a chorus line. When the number was over, I spun back into

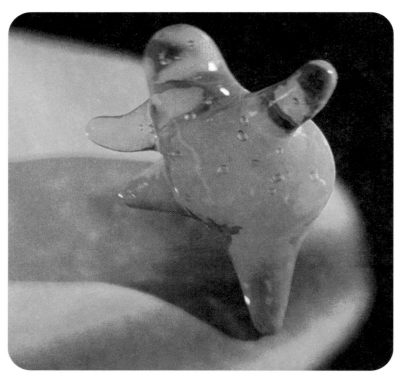

my whole self and bounced out of the light. For the grand finale, Weebo turned on the lawn sprinklers, and they looked like beautiful fountains. They were the perfect backdrop for my dance with myself.

When the music was over, Weebo turned out the lights.

Chapter Six

Weebo Saves the Day

After our party, I was pretty tuckered out. I went to bed willingly.

In the meantime, flying home with the Professor was a less-than-jolly experience. Even though we'd won the game, he was totally down in the dumps.

Why was he so sad? Because of Sara, of course. After the game, he'd tried to talk to her. Alone.

"What you have to say to her," Wilson Croft had snapped, "you can say to both of us. If you can *remember* what you were going to say."

The Professor glared at Wilson and turned to Sara.

"Flubber," he said. "Ring a bell?"

Wilson laughed. "Flubber? Sounds like baby shampoo."

The Professor ignored him. "Sara, you

have to believe me. Flubber won the game."

"What are you talking about?" Sara asked, suspicious.

"The shoes," the Professor explained. "I Flubberized the shoes. That's why they could jump so high."

He didn't even have the chance to finish. She cut him off angrily.

"Are you serious? You're taking credit for Medfield beating Rutland?"

"I'm simply saying that tonight you saw, firsthand, Flubber at work," he explained.

"You're remarkable," she said. She didn't believe him at all. After all, I am fairly incredible.

"I'm telling you the truth, Sara," he said.

"I'm not so sure you know what that is anymore" was her cold reply.

In other words, everything went wrong.

But later that night, Weebo snuck out of the house and visited Sara. She proved to Sara that the Professor really did love her.

That same night, I took Sara and the Professor for a moonlit ride. They both seemed so happy. And you can imagine how shocked Sara was. She'd never thought it possible that a car could fly.

As we soared into the air I could sense her exhilaration. Her mood was catching. It all seemed very magical.

"Well, what do you think?" the Professor asked.

Sara didn't respond.

"Sara?" he prompted.

"This is it," she replied. "This is the solution. This is how we save the school."

"That's what I've been saying," the Professor said, getting all excited. "Imagine the line of shoes we could develop."

"Not shoes, Phillip," Sara explained. "Flight! We have to sell this to an aerospace company."

"Oh. Good idea," he replied.

We pulled into the garage. All was dark, but suddenly there was a glaring light.

The Professor and Sara were frightened. And I could sense the presence of strangers. Not-nice strangers.

I wanted more than anything to bounce away, but I was trapped in the car.

And then I knew who they were! They were the men I kept hitting in the head! Plus one more—their boss, Chester Hoenicker.

"Lovely old car," Hoenicker said. "Mind if I take a look under the hood?"

"Yes, I would," the Professor snapped, his voice shaking.

They ignored him. I got a chill when they raised the hood. There was no telling what they'd do to me.

"It's very simple," Hoenicker said to one of his men. "I expected something more complex."

He paused. "There's a lot of money in your . . . What do you call it? Flubber?"

"Flubber belongs to Medfield College," the Professor declared.

"At the end of the term there isn't going to be a Medfield College," Hoenicker replied.

"We'll see about that," Sara snapped.

Fortunately, they left a few minutes later. But I had a feeling they'd be back.

Chapter Seven

Weebo's Last Stand

The next day, the Professor and Sara and I set out to visit an aerospace corporation. It was somewhere far away—the longest trip we'd ever taken.

Finally we pulled up alongside a tall building and waited. I wondered why we just hovered there like that.

And then someone pulled the curtains back. Sara and the Professor waved like mad, and the humans in the building gaped. At last, the recognition I deserved!

* * *

The part of me still back at the house purred contentedly because I knew everything had gone well. The Professor and Sara were going to save Medfield College. Weebo was watching late-night television upstairs.

Suddenly, two beams of bright white light hit the house. I heard the sounds of wood splintering and glass breaking. Heavy shoes thudded on the basement stairs.

I remained perfectly silent. I'M NOT HERE! I thought. I'M NOT HERE! THERE'S NO ONE HERE!

The two men tore up the basement angrily, smashing everything in their path. And then . . . silence.

A cold hand grabbed a piece of me caught outside the tank. I couldn't help shrieking.

I felt the evil men's satisfaction. They had found me.

Just when I thought I was done for, Weebo popped up out of nowhere. She slammed into one bad guy's head. Then she nailed the other guy.

I didn't stop screeching for a minute. Why couldn't these men just go away and leave us alone?

Finally all was still again, but I knew the men were still there. I could sense their no-good presence.

Weebo scanned the room with her powerful spotlight. The sneaks were hiding.

Weebo found one of them and pegged him in the back of the head.

But then I heard an awful thud, followed by more banging and crashing. The basement was silent again, except for the sound of Weebo's voice. It was faint, and she was saying nonsense over and over, "Dog-cat-mouse-dog-cat-mouse."

And then her voice stopped.

I wailed in agony. Weebo was gone.

Chapter Eight

The Rescue

They loaded me none too gently into the trunk of their black car. Then they drove away—on the road, mind you—very bumpy compared to flying—until we reached a large, scary house.

As I bounced around in the trunk, I kept thinking about Weebo. We'd had such fun together the night of the basketball game. And now I'd never see her again.

When the Professor and Sara got home, they were met with an awful surprise. The

house was a mess, most of me was gone, and Weebo was destroyed. The Professor and Sara guessed exactly what had happened.

The Professor pulled out a gun.

"Phillip! Not a gun!" Sara gasped.

"It's just a squirt gun," he replied.

I sloshed around, trying to tell her I was inside.

"Wouldn't it be better just to call the police?" Sara asked anxiously.

"And tell them what?" the Professor demanded. "I have to deal with this myself," he continued doggedly.

"*We* have to deal with it," Sara corrected.

They got into the car and blasted out of the house. The Professor knew where to go. They headed to the mansion where I was being held prisoner.

Besides the squirt gun, the Professor had brought along a bottle of fluid me. Inside the bottle, I was getting all worked up and excited. And I tingled on the tacks both the Professor and Sara had put on the bottoms of their shoes.

We came to the mansion and landed on the driveway.

The Professor banged on the front door of Hoenicker's house, and one of those evil men appeared.

"I'd like to see Mr. Hoenicker, please," the Professor said, his voice steady. I trembled with anticipation.

The man had a bandage on his head and a cocky grin on his face. I could tell he didn't feel at all bad that he'd hurt Weebo, and he hadn't minded hurting me, either.

We followed him through Hoenicker's lavish house and entered a room where Hoenicker sat grinning contentedly.

The Professor got right to the point of his visit. "I'm prepared to sell you the Flubber."

"Do I really need to *buy* Flubber?" Hoenicker asked.

"Flubber's hard to control," the Professor said, struggling to remain calm.

"My man's working on it," Hoenicker snapped. "It won't be a problem."

I sensed the Professor stiffen.

"I could make it a lot easier for you," the Professor said. "If you give us a thirty-day extension on the loan. Meanwhile, I'll make you as much Flubber as you want."

My blood ran cold at the thought.

"I'll tell you what," Hoenicker said. "I'll give you the thirty days. And you give me two years. Whatever you come up with over the next two years is mine."

"That's not fair!" Sara gasped, outraged.

"Shop somewhere else, lady" was Hoenicker's nasty reply.

"It's all right, Sara," the Professor said soothingly.

"I'll do it," he announced to Hoenicker. "Where's the Flubber?" he added casually.

As we followed one of Hoenicker's men out of the room, the Professor secretly removed the car's remote control device from his pocket. He made the car rise off the driveway and hover outside the library window.

Inside the library, someone was banging

away at a computer keyboard.

"You're going to enjoy this," Hoenicker said to the computer operator.

"Professor," Hoenicker continued, "I got you a little help."

The computer operator stood and turned. I gasped inwardly. It was none other than that creep Wilson Croft.

Wilson smirked. I wanted to whack him right in the face. I got itchy just thinking about it. I started jostling around inside the gun and tingling on the tacks in the Professor's shoes.

I could tell that Sara was shocked and horrified. The Professor seemed more angry than surprised, but he tried not to show it.

"Flubber's very interesting, Phil," Wilson said. "Too bad it's so unstable."

"There's a way to deal with it," the Professor replied, and strode over to my tank.

"Hey!" one of Hoenicker's men shouted, grabbing the Professor's arm. He didn't like the fact that the Professor had taken the bottle of me out of his pocket.

"Hand cream," the Professor explained. "So the Flubber won't stick." I'd never realized what a good liar the Professor could be!

"Let him go," the boss said.

The Professor rubbed me thoroughly over his hands. I tingled with pleasure. It was clear that the Professor's plan—whatever it was— was about to get going.

The Professor tossed the bottle of me over to Sara. She caught it.

"She has to help me," he explained to the others. "Put it on your hands," he told her.

The Professor reached for his other pocket, but the boss's man beat him to it. He pulled out the gun.

"It's a squirt gun," the Professor explained, chuckling.

Hoenicker's man was not amused. He squirted the Professor in the face.

"What's it for?" he growled.

"To lower the temperature of the Flubber," the Professor said. Well, that sounded reasonable enough. Once again, I was impressed by the Professor's lying ability. He was good in a pinch.

Wilson nodded his approval, and the goon gave back the Professor's gun.

Then the Professor placed his hands on my tank locks. The moment I'd been waiting for.

The seal broke with a gush. The others

50

backed away in fear. The Professor lifted the lid and spoke to me softly.

"It's okay. It's me," he said. I knew it was him, of course; I'd known the whole time. Still, it was nice to know he cared. And more than ever I wanted to please him and avenge Weebo's death.

The Professor reached into the tank and slowly drew me out.

"Shh," the Professor ordered. "Everybody be still."

He was coiled like a spring, ready to snap into action. I felt the same way.

There was a moment of unbearable tension as I lay in the Professor's open palm.

"Do it for Weebo," the Professor whispered to me.

I couldn't hold back any longer. I rose

right up out of the Professor's hand.

"Look out!" Wilson screamed.

The Professor hit a button on the car's remote control device. There was a blinding flash of light.

I squealed and took off. I don't know why, but bright light always makes me go berserk.

Hoenicker's henchmen got ready to punch the Professor. But before they could hit him, he jumped high in the air—so high, thanks to the tacks on his shoes, that the guys ended up punching each other in the face instead.

I ricocheted back and forth all over the room, smashing glass and knocking things over. With each shattering sound I got more excited and moved faster and faster until I was just a blur.

Wilson grabbed Sara, and she was so angry at him that she raised her fists—which had liquid me rubbed all over them—and punched him until he toppled over.

"Wow," Sara exclaimed, looking at her fists in amazement.

Then Hoenicker's son charged her, but she jumped out of reach just in time.

One of Hoenicker's goons punched the Professor in the chin, but since his face had me smeared all over it, the man's fist simply bounced away.

"This is fun!" Sara cried, blowing a loose strand of hair out of her face and rolling up her sleeves.

The boss's son grabbed a heavy paper-weight off a table and got ready to heave it. The Professor quickly used the gun to squirt me all over his butt.

When the paperweight came flying at him, he just stuck out his behind. The thing bounced off him and zoomed right back at the horrified kid, whacking him good!

Just then, Sara grabbed me out of the air as I sailed past her. She held me tight.

Wilson sat up, his mouth hanging open. He was still groggy from being hit like a punching bag.

The Professor grabbed Sara and stopped

her from bouncing. She offered me to him, but he shook his head.

"Go ahead," he told her.

She wound up, took aim . . .

"This one's for Weebo," she cried.

With that, she heaved me with all her might. Right at Hoenicker.

He tried to run away, but I was too fast for

him. I nailed him in the back of the head. He went flying out the window, and I went flying back in the other direction.

I landed right in Wilson's open mouth.

"*Ack!*" I cried. It was dark and smelly in there. I simply had to find a way out.

I forced my way through a narrow passage and finally landed in a bigger space filled with sizzling acid. I kept going, and the path got really twisty. Finally, I came to the end of the tunnel. I burst out with all my strength, right through Wilson's pants.

Ah, fresh air.

In the meantime, the Professor and Sara went out onto the balcony and jumped into their getaway car.

I flew out of Hoenicker's ugly house and bounced all the way home.

When I got to the Professor's backyard, I bounded over the fence. I aimed for the bedroom window and made it. I landed right in the Professor's catcher's mitt, which was sitting on a comfy chair.

I breathed a huge sigh of relief. It had been a very busy day.

As I drifted off to sleep, I dreamed of Weebo. She was out there somewhere watching us, and she was happy.

By the way—the Professor and Sara finally got married, and we all lived happily ever after.

Thanks to Weebo.

Notes:

Get Flubber-ized!

Disney's Flubber
0-7868-4136-2
$4.95
AGES 8-12
EIGHT PAGES OF FULL-COLOR
STILLS FROM THE MOVIE

JUNIOR NOVEL

Disney's Flubber
0-7868-3149-9
$14.95
CHOCK-FULL OF FULL-COLOR PHOTOS
FROM THE MOVIE AND FROM BEHIND
THE SCENES

SPECIAL COLLECTOR'S EDITION

Disney's Flubber
0-7868-4200-8
$3.50
AGES 7-9
ILLUSTRATED WITH FULL-COLOR MOVIE
PHOTOS THROUGHOUT

DISNEY CHAPTERS

Available at your local bookstore